D0771365

Snipp, Snapp, Snurr
and the
YELLOW SLED

MAJ LINDMAN

ALBERT WHITMAN & COMPANY
Morton Grove, Illinois

The Snipp, Snapp, Snurr Books
Snipp, Snapp, Snurr and the Buttered Bread
Snipp, Snapp, Snurr and the Gingerbread
Snipp, Snapp, Snurr and the Red Shoes
Snipp, Snapp, Snurr and the Reindeer
Snipp, Snapp, Snurr and the Yellow Sled
Snipp, Snapp, Snurr Learn to Swim

The Flicka, Ricka, Dicka Books
Flicka, Ricka, Dicka and the Big Red Hen
Flicka, Ricka, Dicka and the Little Dog
Flicka, Ricka, Dicka and the New Dotted Dresses
Flicka, Ricka, Dicka and the Three Kittens
Flicka, Ricka, Dicka and Their New Friend
Flicka, Ricka, Dicka Bake a Cake

Library of Congress Cataloging-in-Publication Data
Lindman, Maj.
Snipp, Snapp, Snurr and the yellow sled / by Maj Lindman.
p.   cm.
Summary: Three little Swedish brothers help their mother with
all the chores at home to earn two bright yellow sleds, one for
themselves and one for a poor, unhappy little boy.
ISBN 0-8075-7499-6
[1. Brothers—Fiction. 2. Triplets—Fiction.
3. Family life—Sweden—Fiction.
4. Sweden—Fiction.] I. Title.

PZ7.L659Sny   1995   95-1049
[E]—dc20   CIP
                                            AC

The text is set in 23' Futura Book
and 12' Bookman Light Italic.

A Snipp, Snapp, Snurr Book

The three boys stood looking in the window.

Snipp, Snapp, and Snurr, three little boys who lived in Sweden, were on their way home from school one winter afternoon.

It was snowing hard. Each boy had on his warmest red cap and red sweater, and high brown boots. As they passed a shop window, Snipp said, "Look at that bright yellow sled!"

"It's as yellow as gold," said Snapp.

"It is long enough for three boys just our size to ride on at the very same time," said Snurr. "Look at that steering wheel! Couldn't we have fun!"

The three boys stood looking in the window, each wishing for the bright yellow sled—more than for anything else in the world.

As they turned away from the window and walked slowly down the street, Snapp said, "Let's ask Father to buy it for us."

"You know, it would cost a lot," said Snipp. "Just think how much money he spent for our new winter boots."

"We'd better ask Mother to help us earn it," said Snurr.

"That's a good idea," said Snapp.

"Let's hurry home and ask her," said Snipp.

Snipp, Snapp, and Snurr ran home. They went into the house and straight to the kitchen, where they found Mother drying dishes.

"Mother dear, we have seen a bright yellow sled," said Snipp.

"It's as yellow as gold," said Snapp.

They found Mother drying dishes.

It has a steering wheel," said Snurr, "and it is long enough so we could all ride together."

"How nice!" said Mother, smiling.

"We thought maybe you could tell us a way to earn it," said Snipp.

Mother thought a moment. Then she said, "If you will help me in every way you can for two weeks, I am sure Father and I will feel that you have earned enough money for the sled."

After a long talk it was decided that Snipp should be the first one to get up each morning to put on the teakettle.

Early the next morning Snipp yawned, stretched, and hopped out of bed. He ran to the kitchen and put the teakettle on, thinking all the while about the bright yellow sled.

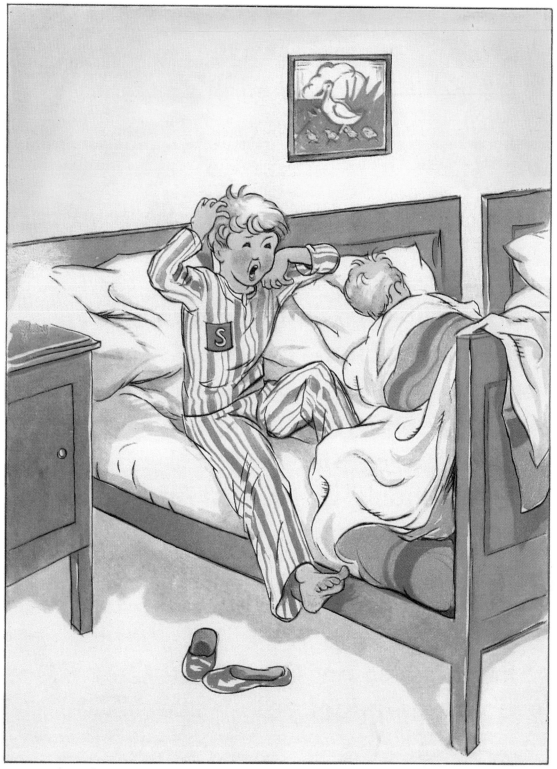

Snipp yawned, stretched, and hopped out of bed.

Snipp, Snapp, and Snurr hurried home from school the next day. They were ready to help Mother.

Snipp sat down to peel the potatoes.

Snapp went to the store with the big market basket to buy all the things on Mother's list.

Snurr stirred the soup on the stove so that it would not burn.

"How glad I am that Snapp has gone to the store," said Mother. "Now I won't have to go out."

As she spoke, Snapp came in the door. The basket he carried was full of packages—tea, sugar, butter, salt. He carried a loaf of bread under his arm.

"When we get the yellow sled we can bring the groceries home on it," said Snapp. "This basket is heavy!"

Snapp came in the door.

Early Saturday morning, Mother asked Snurr to scrub the back stairs. He filled the pail with warm water. He found soap and a scrub brush with a long handle. Then he started up the back stairs.

Perhaps the pail was too full. Perhaps the soap slipped out of his hand and he tried to catch it. Perhaps he only stumbled over the long handle of the brush. But down the stairs he tumbled, with the bucket, brush, soap, and water!

When Mother saw he wasn't hurt, she said, "Never mind, Snurr, all things are hard in the beginning!"

Snapp said, "Well, now the stairs are wet, so your work is half done!"

Snipp helped Snurr wipe the stairs dry after they were scrubbed clean.

But down the stairs he tumbled.

That afternoon Mother said, "Please dust the books in the library. First take each book down from the shelf. Wipe it carefully with this clean, soft cloth. When the shelves are empty, dust them. Then put each book back where you found it."

"What fun!" said Snapp, as he began handing down the books from the highest shelves to Snipp.

Mother left them dusting books and talking about the yellow sled while she went to tea with friends.

When she came home at nearly sunset, she found books everywhere! There were books on the floor and books on the tables and chairs.

Snipp lay flat on the floor reading. Snapp stood near the table reading. Snurr sat on the ladder reading.

Books everywhere!

But the next day, Snipp and Snapp put the books back on the shelves.

Snurr washed the brown stockings that the three boys always wore with their high brown boots.

"My, I didn't know we had so many stockings," said Snurr to himself. The stockings were very dirty.

Snurr got the washboard. He used plenty of soap. He rubbed the stockings hard, up and down.
He rubbed them on the right side.
He turned them and washed them carefully on the wrong side. Then he washed out all the soap and water and hung them up to dry.

"I must tell Snipp and Snapp not to get mud on their stockings," he said to himself.

He rubbed the stockings hard, up and down.

The very first day of the week was Mother's birthday. Snipp, Snapp, and Snurr hurried home from school.

Snipp rushed out to buy flowers. Snapp put the teakettle on to make tea. Snurr placed the birthday cake which Father had bought on the cake plate.

When Snipp came home with the flowers, he said, "Let's go in now to wish Mother happy birthday."

"You go first with the flowers," said Snapp. "I'll come next with the tea. Snurr can carry the birthday cake."

Snipp opened the door.

"Happy birthday, Mother!" said the three little boys.

"This is indeed a happy birthday!" replied Mother.

Snipp opened the door.

One bright Saturday morning, Mother said, "You boys have helped me in every way I have asked. You have earned the yellow sled. Shall we go to the store today?"

"Yes, let's!" said Snipp.

"That's fine, Mother!" said Snapp.

"Thank you," Snurr quickly added.

Mother put on her hat and coat. The three boys had their warmest red caps and red sweaters. Of course they wore their high boots.

Then they all went down the street to the shop where the yellow sled was for sale.

When they reached the store, Mother went in. Snipp, Snapp, and Snurr stood outside, looking in the window.

Then they all went to the shop.

Just think, it's ours!" said Snipp.

"Won't we have fun?" said Snapp.

"It's worth all the work," said Snurr.

Suddenly the boys heard a sound. They turned to look. Near the window stood a little boy. He was crying.

"What's the matter?" asked Snipp.

"I want that sled so very much," he said. "I've never had a sled."

"Won't your father buy you a sled?" asked Snapp.

"He can't," answered the boy. "We don't have enough money."

Snipp turned to Snapp and Snurr. "What about giving him our yellow sled?" he asked.

Near the window stood a little boy.

He's too little to earn enough money for a sled," said Snapp.

Mother came out of the shop. "Here is your sled, Snipp, Snapp, and Snurr," she said.

The boys looked at each other. Then Snipp said, "Mother, we are big boys."

"Yes," said Snapp, "we are big boys, and we have learned to work."

"Mother," said Snurr, "may we work to earn another sled? We would like to give ours to this little boy."

When Mother understood, she took all four boys to the top of a snowy hill.

Snipp, Snapp, and Snurr helped the little boy get on the sled. Then Snapp gave him a push—and away he went on the bright yellow sled!

Away he went on the bright yellow sled!

What fun the boys had on the hillside. "Thank you! Oh, thank you," said the little boy after every ride. "My brothers and sisters thank you, too. We will have such good times. That bright yellow sled will be the most wonderful thing we've ever had."

At last the three boys and Mother went home. Snipp, Snapp, and Snurr went to work to earn a second bright yellow sled.

For the next two weeks, when the three boys were doing all the things that Mother asked, one would say to the other, "Do you remember how happy that little boy looked on the bright yellow sled?"

And Snipp, Snapp, and Snurr were happy, too.

Each boy went to work.

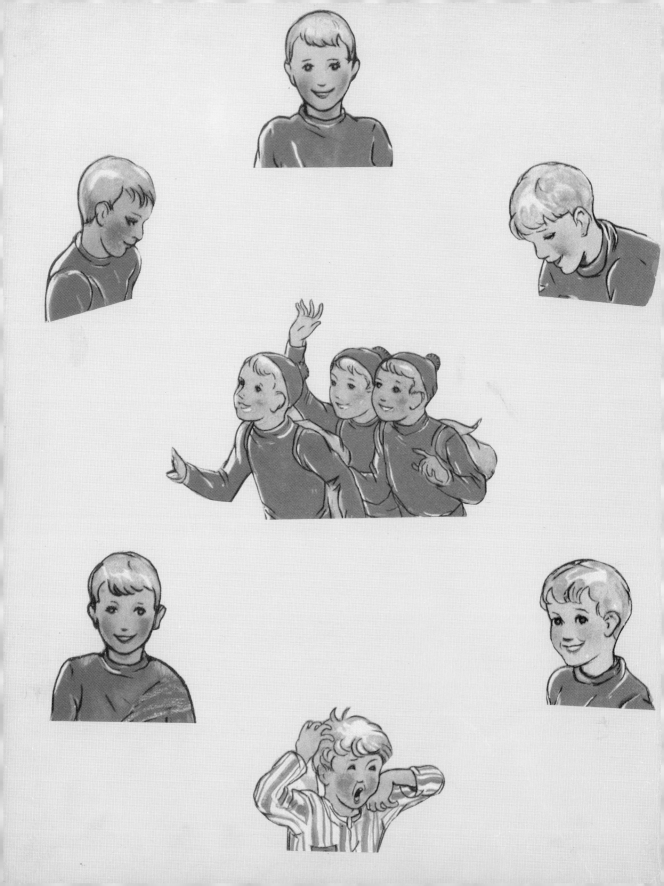